INSANE *Joy*

WOODROW ODOM LUCAS

PublishAmerica
Baltimore

First printing

ISBN: 1-4241-9920-4
PUBLISHED BY PUBLISHAMERICA, LLLP
www.publishamerica.com
Baltimore

Printed in the United States of America

DEDICATION

This book is dedicated to my wife of ten years, Machel Leanne Mills Lucas, who no matter how bad things got, never stopped believing in me.

ACKNOWLEDGMENTS

I would like to acknowledge all of my friends and family who supported me through the process of creating this book to include, but not limited to, Gerald Lucas, Melba Lucas, Gerald Lucas, Jr., Autumn Lucas, Christophe Ringer, Christian Straugn, Dante Bryant, and Malik Saafir. I would especially like to acknowledge Lynn the Sage and my grandma, Clementine Odom, whose prayer, wisdom, support, and encouragement have made me into the man that I am today.

INTRODUCTION

In the hustle of a world that had forsaken nature, Grandfather Jacob sat with his Grandson Joseph.

"Grandaddy," Joseph said, "the kids pick on me, and I have these strange dreams and I'm afraid to go outside during the day."

Grandfather Jacob responded, "Joseph, don't let it get you down, 'cause you got a God who will love you till the end of all time and beyond that!"

Joseph got angry and said, "Grandaddy, what do you know? Look at your life. You got it all. What do you know about suffering?"

And his hrandfather said, "Son, sit down for a moment and let me show you a story about some of Grandaddy's suffering." The grandfather went to his bookshelf and took out a notebook that had "A Dream of Insanity" on the front. He said to his grandson, "Now read this, my boy, and you will know of overcoming, then we'll pray about some of those issues of yours and get you some help. But first you must get hope, for hope is the adversity killer."

The boy was dejected and despondent but had been taught to obey his elders, so he took the notebook and began to read.

CHAPTER 1
SCREWING THE POOCH

Hey, how ya doin'? My name is Jacob Forthworthy and I'm a writer. Well, in actuality, I'm just an aspiring writer. I'm also crazy by the way. You see, I'm a graduate student at Dream University and I am stark-raving mad. I mean, I don't mean gunning down a bunch of folks at McDonald's crazy, but I do mean like hearing voices, having a suicidal thought or two, having weird physical afflictions that I can't grasp, and having a really hard time some mornings, afternoons, and evenings getting out of bed crazy. Not only am I crazy on nominal levels, but having been diagnosed with schizoaffective disorder in 2001, I'm officially out of my mind! This is my story.

Where do I begin? Well, I suppose with right now, then I'll go backwards, and end again, right now. So here I am. Once again I have screwed the pooch on a job and find myself unemployed. It was just a summer internship, but still the shame and guilt of screwing something up remain. Am I a screw-up or just misunderstood? Not sure. You be the judge. Anyway, sometimes I think that they screwed the pooch because it was a pretty chaotic situation. Was it them, was it me, is it us? Who knows? All I know is that I am once again unemployed, so I figured I'd write a book. But who am I? I'm certainly not famous, nor have I done anything that most people would view as important. But I'm crazy. Yeah, I most certainly am crazy. And shouldn't that be enough?

So back to screwing the pooch. I did it for real this time. I was forced to resign for the second time in my career. You should have seen the first time; I was really crazy then. I would go into the bathroom and pray prayers at the top of my lungs and then come out like no one heard me. I was convinced that no one heard me! How about that? Paper thin walls, screaming to Jesus at the top of my lungs, and I actually thought that no one heard? Now that's crazy!

I suppose this time around, my biggest problem was sitting still. Every time I would try and sit for any long period of time, I would feel affliction in my stomach, hear voices, or have to use the bathroom. So I was always out of my seat. And that was bad 'cause I sat right by the president of the company and you know how visual people are. I did good work, though. I created cool PowerPoints and spreadsheets, but appearances, baby. They're big. I mean, I already had a strike against me 'cause I'm crazy and people can sense that. When you couple that with just roaming around the building constantly, people start to talk.

To be totally honest, I wasn't really forced to resign the second time around, I just did so on my own accord. Mostly because I was so paranoid on the job that I simply couldn't function. I know it isn't in vogue nowadays to talk about Satan or dark forces, especially when you suffer from mental illness, but in one week both my cars broke down, one of my best friends was arrested for armed robbery, and I caught hell on the job. Now this was not that big a deal, but at least enough to spur enough paranoia to end my summer tenure.

But I'm getting nowhere just talking about how I screwed the pooch. I mean, you didn't pay $12.99 to hear a story of mundane incompetence. So let me just start at the beginning, my birth and then go forward. But I'll have to go pretty fast through the first parts because how interesting can a birth be? And to be honest, my memory is kind of limited so I don't remember much anyway. Memory loss is a really inconvenient symptom of mental illness. But don't look for a lot of cool facts like in *The Noonday Demon*. Why? I just told you that I can't remember much, so how the heck can I remember really cool facts like one in ten people shave their legs. Anyway, I'll gloss over the beginning parts, and then I'll get to the juicy parts about when my illness really started flaring up. I mean that stuff is awesome, straight up nail-biter type material.

CHAPTER 2
THE STEPFORD SUBURB

Okay, here we are, at my birth. I was born in Destined City in 1974. Yeah, I'm pretty old, a whopping 32 almost. Anyway, when I was one year old my parents moved to a small, predominantly white, suburb that sort of reminds one of the Stepford wives. This is important information because, you see, my mother grew up in the racist South and was quite a militant. Consequently, she didn't take too kindly to the "Stepford" trappings of lake membership and fake, condescending, suburbanite smiles.

From a very young age, I had predilections toward illness. I would often imagine that the clown painting in my room was going to attack me, or I would wake up in the middle of the night and imagine snakes in my room. But I and my parents just attributed these things to overactive imagination. Among the things in Stepford that I didn't imagine were two misplaced parents who were constantly fighting, a maladjusted and somewhat persecuted brother who couldn't stand the town, always acting as if everything was a joke because reality seemed ridiculous, and second grade teachers accusing me of stealing raincoats from classmates half my size. Not to mention black classmates who thought I was a "crossover" because I listened to Credence Clearwater Revival. What can I say, I love the classics.

Needless to say, Stepford was not exactly the most nurturing environment for a young African-American male, but I suppose if you

12

compare it to the Ida B. Wells housing project, it had its merits. I got a great education and good opportunities. Unfortunately for a predilection toward mental illness, I also got a maladjusted and misinformed sense of identity with which I am just now beginning to come to grips.

So I promised you that I would gloss over the beginning parts and in a nutshell that is my childhood. It was normally abnormal to coin a phrase and really not very interesting either, so on to bigger and better things.

Chapter 3
The Omen

In the midst of profligate avoidance and cowardice throughout my childhood, much of which in retrospect I believe stemmed from illness, I was able to accomplish some things. I was a merit semi-finalist and co-captain of my football team. As a result, I was somewhat sought after by several college football "neardowells." Well, in actuality only one pretty prestigious university recruited me directly. A military academy was recruiting my cousin Sim, who, by the way, ran a 4.4 second 40-yard dash. Unfortunately, though his body was aptly suited for football, his mind was more focused on Catholic monasticism and Zen Buddhism. Long story short, the military school got the both of us in a package deal. This military school to cynics is like a thirteenth year of high school, but for us athletes was more like a red shirt freshman year, since the military academies at that time didn't red shirt their freshmen.

Military life was both an awakening and a death. For the first time in my life, I really saw the positive effects of discipline. Though I was third string on the football team, I academically performed toward the top of my class for two out of three quarters. Then came Daytona Beach, Florida. I remember my cousin Sim, who matured a little earlier in Christ than myself, saying, "Jacob, you can't always operate on the extreme. You're a top student; you can't operate on the social extreme as well." Of course, being the good Episcopalian that I was

(Episcopalians are high on compassion and mercy but low on moral discipline), I told him to screw himself and got "fucked up" as much as possible.

Well, one such occasion was on spring break in Daytona Beach, Florida. I scored some high-grade acid and tripped for three and a half straight days. This was my first experience with real illness. I mean I was loopy. And for the next three to five months, I heard voices and had headaches. Of course I confided this to no one, as I didn't really think much of it at the age of 18. Unfortunately, I decided that I couldn't withstand the rigors of playing football at the academy in that condition and thus ended my military career.

The fact that the effects of the acid took so long to wear off was ominous, as in an omen of things to come. Hence the chapter title, "The Omen." Of course, I also picked up a tinge of self-righteousness and unforgiveness while in the military ranks, which would not bode favorably for future trials. I will address these things further in future chapters. But for now, suffice it to say that my military experience reflected the beginnings or perhaps reinforcement of true duality, inspiration on one side and illness on the other.

CHAPTER 4
FRESHMAN FROLICKS

During the summer between my year in the military and the following school year, I was able to get into university. Don't ask me how it happened, it just did. In retrospect, I see the Lord's hand in it, but for those who are not religiously inclined, just call it serendipity. Anyway, my freshman year at university was fantastic. I was very popular with the ladies and for the first time in my life, I felt accepted by my own race. For the first time in my life I had some black male friends with whom I did not have to prove my manhood or blackness. These young brothers accepted me for what I was and had the intellectual capacity to know that I was just as tough as anyone else whether I liked Phil Collins or not. And yet there were still headaches and a kind of anger that was inexplicable.

But shit didn't really hit the fan until Christmas break. My parents finally decided to move out of Stepford to the Midwest of all places. Socio-culturally that was like going from the frying pan into the fire, but I was no longer at home, so I suppose it didn't matter much. Well, my first major accomplishment of Christmas break was wrecking our Toyota Camry. My father said, "Watch this turn, it's tough." And of course before I could get "I know, Dad" out of my mouth, we were in a ditch. My father was furious. But I just laughed a strange laughter. It was a mixture of shame, guilt, resentment, rage, and rebellion. Maybe I was laughing in rage at the idiocy of a boy who allows others to call him nigger and get away with it. Or perhaps I was laughing at the irony of a kid who defended his race instead of himself and carried the success of his people on his shoulders. I am not sure, but I laughed nonetheless. This of course did detriment to my relationship with my father, reifying in his mind the impression that I was an irresponsible derelict. A judgment that on the one hand was completely erroneous when one considered my 3.9 at university, but was totally justified when one considered my profligate forty drinking and random attacks on white students on campus.

Well, my mother was still in Stepford, my brother was at college, living it up, and my father had to travel that break on business. So I was in the crib by my lonesome. Wouldn't you know that paranoia would set in something fierce. I mean I was scared of my own shadow. Of course at the time I thought that it was just fear and cowardice and so in my shame, I did not confide any of my emotions to anyone else. I just sat in the house watching TV and eating Ritz crackers.

One night, *Ben Hur* came on. There was this scene where Ben Hur's leprosy-ridden sisters encountered Jesus' shadow and were healed. Well, for no known reason, I was so overcome with emotion at the beauty of the event that I broke out in tears, threw up my hands, looked to the ceiling, and screamed at the top of my lungs, "My whole life is yours!" After this, I called my born-again Christian friend and said, "Hope, something strange just happened! I'm not quite sure what, but it was surely something!"

In retrospect, that was a salvific encounter. Even though I had been confirmed at age 11 and took communion my whole life, that was the moment at which I comprehended Jesus on a deeper level. That was also a strange turning point in the illness.

When I came back to school, I started feeling these strange inexplicable pains in my stomach. Deliverance ministers have often told me that I opened the door to the demonic when I tripped on acid. So maybe these pains were the Holy Spirit getting rid of demonic energy. I'm really not sure; all I know is that they were on me.

When I came back to university I also changed girlfriends and became abusive for the first time in my life. I was never physically abusive, but verbally, I spoke with a venom that just didn't seem to match my personality. Maybe it was rage again from being passed over as a youngster. But why did it all of a sudden start afflicting me? I just didn't understand it. Needless to say, although the girl I started dating was a truly incredibly person, the relationship was a nightmare and we both had to move on. The next girl I met would eventually become my wife, but that is another chapter altogether.

CHAPTER 5
JUNIOR CRISIS

My sophomore year at university was incredible. I met my wife-to-be, a relationship of healing, betrayal, and love, which I will save for another book altogether. Especially when one considers that I was not truly faithful to her until we got married three years later. I was granted acceptance to this pretty competitive program and thrived within its auspice. Things went really well that year. I worked out regularly and was involved in this initiative to get Asian-American studies implemented at university. Things didn't get fuzzy again until my junior year.

Junior year was a strange year. I broke up with my girlfriend. We would break up three more times before finally getting married at the end of my senior year. I was simply off balance. I was drinking and imbibing in marijuana more than usual and I had this strong conviction toward social justice. My living situation was problematic and my grades were beginning to suffer. I finally took off the spring quarter of my senior year to write a book entitled, *A Book of Rhythm*, which finally got published a couple of years back. It was a book that was full of rage and venom, plea and agony, healing and forgiveness.

Writing the book was therapeutic but it also marked a strange turning point. After writing the book, my penchant for marijuana was altogether gone. This is probably due to the fact that I had committed some of my worst sins while under the influence of marijuana, and I simply concluded that I just couldn't hold my "jeeba." Some folks can't handle liquor, but for me it was marijuana. In any event, I was much closer to God after writing the book, which is not necessarily always a good thing, given the nature of our society.

When I returned to school, I reconnected with my girlfriend and our relationship was amazing. But there was an ominous call toward God. A call toward God that would eventually be my undoing. A call toward God that would not be denied. A reckless love of the Lord that would one day lead me to a cross that I never thought possible. But that's for a later couple of chapters.

Chapter 6
Rapid Engagement

All right, here's a little something about my wife. I dated my wife for three years during college. Unfortunately, while I have been completely faithful in marriage, I was not the most loyal or devoted boyfriend. I was young and had a lot of problems with identity so I drank and sought after trouble whenever I could. My wife, ironically, accepted me just as I was. She didn't force me to be "corporate" or "gangsta" or "conservative" or "liberal" or "Christian," labels and categories that have never really suited me. She accepted me for who I was. Unfortunately, given my background of distrust and betrayal, it took me much longer to learn to truly unconditionally reciprocate that acceptance.

In any event, my wife and I got engaged at the end of my senior year at university. To be honest, I think that asking her to marry me was my way of saying, "You're the best person I've ever met, I love you and I don't want to lose you, so let's get married." Unfortunately, as flattering as that statement may be, it is not the same statement as, "Baby, I love you. I am mature enough to commit myself wholly to you. Let's make a life together." I believe that deep down I knew that no matter how much I loved Machel, I wasn't ready for marriage, which is why my plan was for a long engagement.

But the night that my wife and I got engaged, we got caught up in the moment and became careless. As a result, a month after we got engaged, my wife informed me that she was pregnant. Needless to say, having been brought up in a pretty Judeo-Christian setting and wanting to maintain at least the facade of sexual propriety, my wife and I got married shortly after we found out that she was pregnant.

Now, our marriage in the beginning was not marital bliss; marital nightmare is more like it. As soon as I found that she was pregnant, the reality of marriage hit me and connected the disconnect between my subconscious and conscious minds. For up until that moment, romance kept my subconscious knowledge blissfully separate from my conscious delusion. Bottom line, marriage and family meant that I had to find a way to survive in a world that I had judged as unworthy of my time.

At the time that I got married, I felt a strong call to the prophetic and mystical. I saw the evils of greed and malice in our society and had a strong conviction to live "counter" or alternative to the "consciousness" that many label as the American dream. Now I had pretty much carved out a way to do that for just myself or even for my wife and I, but a totally innocent creature that I had to serve and protect while raging my war against American myopia was a bit overwhelming. And so the best thing to ever happen to *me*, the birth of my daughter, was simultaneously the worst thing that could have happened to *my illness*.

Chapter 7
Autumn, the Season of Joy

My daughter is a genius. She is precocious, sensitive, and empathic. She says things like, "Daddy, why are you always talking bad about white people?" I remember going through the first really long depression of my life during the first months of my marriage to Machel. But one of my proudest moments in life was coaching my wife through natural childbirth and seeing the fruits of mostly her, but a wee bit of my, labor.

I used to sing my daughter songs like, "Autumn, Autumn God's coming down for his kingdom, Autumn Autumn God's coming down for you." These songs would remind me of the fact that I had a life to protect and care for that did not choose my life path or obstacles. I mean my daughter did not choose to follow a prophetic life in Christ. My daughter did not choose to have a father with bipolar or schizoaffective disorder. My daughter did not choose to commit herself to helping the less fortunate when she was in my wife's womb. As a result, my torment over getting sick has been high, precisely because of the daughter and wife that it was affecting more so than the illness itself.

Balancing Christ's call and family is hard for anyone. Because a wise man once told me, God demands that his chosen jump seven feet, irrespective of what burdens, responsibilities, or joys that we choose for our self. So God gets his seven feet, whether a nigga has a family or not. And trust me, that seven feet is a lot higher than it seems when we start the journey. But again, managing the call to ministry and a family was dynamite for the illness that stirred within me.

CHAPTER 8
THE BLOOD, THE BLOOD

The only entities in the universe more dynamic than the blood of Jesus are the Creator, the Holy Ghost, and Jesus himself. The blood saves, sanctifies, and it clarifies. I grew up Episcopalian. Episcopalians are big on mercy and compassion but they leave concepts like the blood for fascist fundamentalists and Baptists. As a result, when I encountered the notion that Christ atoned for our sins on the cross and that his shed blood enables us to be justified before the Creator and to become daughters and sons of God, I was both overjoyed and horrified. Needless to say, being introduced to the "blood" introduced yet another inner conflict into my life. On the one side, I was full of indescribable joy, which inexplicably stemmed from simply receiving the testimony of Christ's loving atonement, yet I was horrified by the notion that all who did not receive and subsequently accept this message would burn in eternal torment.

Postponing the schizophrenia of "limited atonement" theology for another chapter, let me focus on joy. Joy is a dangerous thing, for it is truly supernatural. I mean contrary to secular belief, joy is not the same things as happiness. Happiness is a great emotion, and to be honest because of its stable nature I often prefer it to joy. But joy is like touching the face of the divine with one's inner being. It is similar to Bodhichita enlightenment or the face of the divine within one's inner being. It is similar to Bodhichita compassion or nirvana. In a state joy, an individual can often tell people things about themselves that they didn't know that anyone else knew. Joy is the most pervasive physical manifestation that stems from an awareness of the living water of the Holy Spirit.

In a phrase, once I accepted the "blood," I became addicted to joy. This probably stemmed from preferring an a-sober state of prophetic enlightenment to the depression and "stinky thinking" that often defined my condition prior.

In any event, the problem with being addicted to joy is that is serves as an escape from the reality of stable emotion and consciousness. I mean whatever would give me joy, whether it was fasting (I fasted on orange juice for 40 days twice in the same year, which was not exactly the most mind-stabilizing activity) or evangelizing or giving homeless people twenty dollar bills, if I thought it would bring me joy, I was definitely doing it. Now number one, that's not theologically sound because God calls us to seek righteousness and not joy, and number two, given the fact that I was married and not single, this whole Christian mystic lifestyle that I was trying to live simply was not going to cut it. Similarly, for a person who struggles with imbalance, there is a fine line between "joy" and "mania," and while I was undiagnosed at the time, I believe that I crossed that line several times in chasing the "blood-induced crack cocaine of unlimited ecstasy."

CHAPTER 9
ETERNAL PARANOIA

All right, here we go, time for "limited atonement theology" lesson 101. Sounds complicated, doesn't it? Limited atonement theology rolls off the tongue like hermeneutics or exegesis. In reality limited atonement theology isn't really strange at all. In fact, most conservative Christian religion is founded on some version of it. Limited atonement is the Calvinistic notion that when Christ died on the cross, he only died for certain people and the entire population wasn't included in the subset for whom he sacrificed his life. I know, I know, sounds crazy, right? Well, not really. Most conservative Christian religions believe that Christ died for all of humanity, yet they also believe that only a certain number of individuals will actually be saved. The fundamental problem with this is if God is sovereign and all powerful and foreknows and predestines all things, then how can only a few people make it into Heaven if it is God's will that all go there? Consequently, a reasonable conclusion to draw is that Christ didn't really die for all humanity, but he really died for those who he foreknew and predestined.

Now although I believe that most cnservative Christians believe this "limited atonement" theology on a subconscious level, on the conscious level this notion is anathema to must of us. I mean, we are huge on choice and God-like preordaining certain people to torment is just totally incomprehensible. Yet in reality this is the only stable conclusion we can draw, aside from the notions that those of us who

27

believe in Jesus are like supermen and superwomen who can only "save" a few others or that none will eternally perish because God is all loving and all merciful. If we can't believe that people are going to eventually make it in the end, then if we truly care about our human brothers and sisters, we inevitably fall into a state of "eternal paranoia."

Eternal paranoia is the state of consciousness where we fear for the eternal fate of any person anywhere at all times. Eternal paranoia results in conducting compulsive evangelism almost everywhere we go. When we truly think that it is up to us, instead of up to God, then we end up bearing a burden that the conscious mind simply cannot stomach. Long story short, I fell deeply into "eternal paranoia" when I bought into the conservative ideology of eternal damnation. Eternal paranoia is the condition that probably led me to the brink of psychotic break, and I can honestly say that I do not believe that I would have as much progress out of illness had I not traded the notion of eternal damnation for the notion of universal atonement, but again, that is for another chapter.

CHAPTER 10
A PRISON OF HOLINESS

It was a hot summer morning in August of 1999. I had spent the summer evangelizing with abandon, fasting, praying over my daughter, arguing with my wife, letting several homeless people live with me, getting rejected by most of the people I evangelized to, engaging in heavy spiritual warfare, working at the City League, and attempting to discern the Lord's voice. This last activity is of major importance.

Now although I was Baptist, I had a strong interest in all things "charismatic." Charismatic Christianity is that "crazy" religion where people actually believe in the miraculous ability of God to literally heal people and the miraculous ability of God to perform all sorts of miracles in this modern day and age. Many of these individuals believe that not only can one have an awareness of God, but that one can actually audibly hear God's voice. Ironically, even after all that has happened, I still have a tremendous amount of respect for charismatics and still tenuously hold to the notion that God can miraculously heal and that God talks to us. It's just that now that I realize my own limitations, I am a lot more suspicious of all things "voice" related than I used to be.

The morning of August 1999 was my first full-time day of work at the City League. I had been working at the City League part-time since February of the same year when I needed a way to supplement my income while in seminary. My job at the City League was incredible. It was a dream job. I made good money, I was helping out in the community, it was the perfect complement to ministry, and my boss loved me. And yet for some reason on the morning of August 1999 I was filled with dread and ominous foreboding. I was full of questions and internal statements that didn't logically cohere. "Could I put in a full day's work? Why didn't anyone at my job like me? They all judged me because I wasn't ghetto enough! They are all too liberal about God's word! These evil liberals talking about the goodness of other religions, they're all going to hell! I don't have time to be working for Caesar, I have the work of God to take care of! I must save people from hell!" For some reason on one morning in August of 1999, I was full of judgment and doubt.

The summer had not been easy. I had wrestled with the sickness of my grandmother; I had wrestled with ungrateful people who took my ministry for granted, I had wrestled with pastors who were more conservative than I was, and friends who were more liberal. My wife was tired of the fasts and the constant warfare, my family had very little understanding of the path that I was on, and I was simply generally fed up with all things life oriented. Also, my relationship with some young brothers that I had been working with for about a year and a half seemed to be deteriorating. In the beginning of the relationship these boys would come over to our crib and watch *Cinderella* and we would take them around town with us. But lately, there was a lot of conflict. I had given them a bike to share and it got stolen. And for some reason, even though one of the most stupid things that I could have done is give a bike with no lock on it to some kids living in the projects, I blamed the boys for the loss of the bike. In a phrase, "I was all fucked up!" And on one morning in August of 1999, Satan came a-knocking!

During that summer, in addition to experiencing a type of early life crisis, I was also toying with going into this place called the High Holy Mission. The High Holy Mission is a fundamentalist mission that concentrates on helping homeless people. I thought that serving in a place like the Mission would bring me much closer to God. And yet I also knew that no one in my life would support such an endeavor.

I had talked to my wife about it, and she was ambivalent about us going in.

On one hot morning in August, I got up and got into my 1987 Camaro. I was tense and pensive. I got to work early and said my hellos. I endured the morning; it was basically uneventful. I had to give a presentation that week about the math tutoring enrichment work that I did that summer with some neighborhood children. I was nervous because I was positive that God was going to ensure that I looked stupid. Why I was positive of this forthcoming humiliation, I cannot conjecture, especially when I did impeccable work that summer. In any event, I left for lunch and began to hear voices saying, "Go to the mission, go to the mission!" Then I saw one of the boys whom I mentored while driving around on my lunch break. I picked him up and then felt this surge of panic. Should I just hang out with this kid all day? Should I go back to work? In that moment, I made perhaps the most life-changing decision of my short tenure on this earth. I dropped the boy off at his house and made my way to the mission. I parked outside the mission, went inside to the recruitment person, and said, "I want to join up!"

He immediately inducted me, had me sign an oath to God that I would stay for at least 60 days, and gave me a new set of clothes to wear and a Bible. In that instant, I felt a crushing weight from within and from outside, almost like I was hit with a blunt instrument. I felt as though something was trying to steal my mind and my thoughts. My teeth suddenly went numb. I felt amazing amounts of shame and humiliation at simply leaving my job without telling anyone where I was going. I felt shame and humiliation at leaving my wife and daughter without telling them where I was going. And yet this was something that I felt I had to do.

In the subsequent weeks, I was tormented by strange physical sensations, fears that I couldn't comprehend, horrible nightmares, and an estrangement with almost everyone in my life. My wife found me in the mission, at which point I asked her to come in with me. She refused. She told me that I had betrayed her and our daughter. My brother told me that I was a spoiled child. My father told me that I was running away and that things would be worse when I got out than they were when I got in. And my mother told me that I had lost my mind. In retrospect, I believe that my mother was probably closest to reality.

In any event, the mission was probably better than it seemed as my state of mind at the time accentuated its negative qualities. But it was austere to say the least. There was this bench where one had to sit like a child when one broke one of the rules. And there was a pervasive fear that ran through the entire establishment. I remember feeling this unbelievable rage that grown men were being treated like children just because they had fallen on hard times, or drug addiction, or mental illness. Still the mission got the "special" ones good-paying jobs. My memory of the mission can be summarized in one phrase: "More fear than I have ever felt in my life."

The truth is that when I left the mission after 60 days of service, my dad was right: things were much worse than they were when I went in, for I was afraid of my own shadow. I felt these strange physical afflictions constantly. While in the mission, I had invented a prayer style called the forgiving of sins prayer style, which I use to this day as a way to try and free myself from the insanity that I could feel warring about in my members. But this prayer style was no match for what I was experiencing. I felt an immeasurable weight at all times, strange, horrible temptations that I had never felt before, and so much pain that I wished for death constantly. I remember one afternoon while working for a temp agency, as I was not functional enough to return to my job at the City League, I went to the bathroom and went numb all over. I remember breaking into tears of joy as I thought that it was the angel of death coming to end my misery. I had no affection for my wife, my daughter, my family. I felt nothing for anyone; all I wanted was an end to the pain that I felt on a physical, mental, emotional, and spiritual level.

CHAPTER 11
THE HOUSE OF USHER

After six months of struggling after leaving the mission, I had to acknowledge that I was no longer functional enough to lead my family. One of the ironies of my condition was that I was also not functional enough to seek any type of help. Many times, the mentally ill and demonically oppressed fail to seek help out of fear and dysfunction more so than pride and obstinacy. The only people that I was able to even remotely open up to about the nature of what I was experiencing were my parents. As a result, in March of the year 2000, at the age of 25 years old, I moved back in with my parents.

Now, the fact that I was able to confide illness to my parents is a testimony to the fact that despite their faults, they had successfully imparted a sense of trust and honesty in their children. Unfortunately, they had very little understanding of mental illness at the time. And so our collective household, consisting of my wife, my daughter, myself, my mother, and my father, was to say the least dysfunctional. In fact dysfunction doesn't even begin to scratch the surface of the resentment, pain, rebellion, confusion, and general ill-will that was felt by all parties for all other parties.

Throughout all of this, I still did not seek any form of professional assistance, assuming that if I just prayed hard enough, God would get me through the situation. Of course the presumption of such a perspective involves assuming that one actually grasps the full gravity of one's condition. Luckily, I got a wake-up call later that year in the winter of 2001.

CHAPTER 12
IMMANUEL GOD WITH US

After almost a year of living with my parents my relationship with my wife really deteriorated as did my relationship with my parents. I was totally dysfunctional, yet maintaining a job to make ends meet and assuage the internal perception that I was a 26-year-old, free-loading failure. To claim some kind of control of over my marital situation, I decided to go on a no-food, no-water marriage fast. I started it in January of 2001. Needless to say, given the unstable nature my condition, the fast was not the best decision that I have ever made. Shortly after I started the fast, I found myself unable to function at my job and I up and quit one day when I couldn't think of a response to a caller who needed assistance. I was so frustrated with my condition that I just up and quit.

When I went home to tell my father the news, to say the least, he was unhappy. Our interaction that evening escalated into a full-blown ten-day psychotic break in which I was convinced of several delusions including the idea that my wife and parents were robots, my daughter was a demon sent by the devil to torment me, I was professor Xavier of the X-Men, I was the whore of Babylon about to give birth to a giant spider, and killer spiders were about to attack the planet Earth. After ten days of delusional dysfunction such as not eating or sleeping and stealing the cars ad-nausem, my wife tricked me into going to the hospital.

The first doctor I spoke with subtly accused me of drug abuse and flippantly told my wife that I had bipolar disorder and would be on medication for the rest of my life. My time in the hospital reminded me of the High Holiness Mission. I felt trapped in the hospital and my only desire was to leave. So I was overjoyed when my insurance company refused to cover outpatient care with the hospital and also refused to cover any further stay therein. Though my presiding, second, doctor, a very nice man, said that he would need more time to give me an air-tight diagnosis, the consensus at my departure was schizoaffective, a cross between schizophrenia and bipolar. As I told you, I'm not giving you a lot of facts, so go to crazymeds.org or just Google it to look up the symptoms of schizoaffective.

Shortly after my release, I experienced momentary elation but quickly fell into depression. I saw a few psychiatrists who assured me that I had permanently damaged myself and would never be the same again. They also assured me that my intellect was permanently damaged and to quote one in particular, "Well, he'll never go to Harvard!" Oh, just to digress, I do in fact plan to go to Harvard either as a visiting professor or a student, but that's for another chapter. So to summarize, my psychotic break was really a blessing in disguise because it prompted me to finally seek professional help. Yet before recovering, I would first have to overcome the devastating pessimism, hopelessness, myopia, and manipulation of most of the mental health community.

CHAPTER 13
FATHER'S FUNERAL

While I promised myself that this book would be as a-political as possible so as not to alienate anyone, I have to briefly state that there seems to at least be a tacit connection between the proverbial foot on our collective necks, the societal norms that do not allow us to show or express emotion, and the undiagnosed mental illness that plagues a significant number of black men. One such black man who went undiagnosed his entire life was my father-in-law. My father-in-law, who was by far one of the most prophetic and sensitive men that I have ever met, shot himself in the head in March of the year 2001 while I was just beginning to come to grips with my own pathology. He shot himself in the midst of a delusional episode, which was brought about by among other things the alcoholism that had plagued him for several years.

Now this news was especially devastating to my wife who had also lost her older brother to a boating accident in 1997. So of course she needed a fair share of support. Well, in March of 2001 my functionality literally consisted of forcing myself to accompany my wife to the grocery store to purchase adult diapers for when I wetted myself. So to say the least, I was pretty inept in the moral support department.

The funeral was a nightmare only paralleled by the Mission debacle. I felt alienated, paranoid, was constantly wishing that either I or all of the other people there would suddenly drop dead, thus putting me out of my misery. Given my pain, I was totally self-absorbed and ill-equipped to comfort a woman who was going through arguably the most difficult experience of her life. I hated everyone around me and constantly fantasized about escaping to Europe and living in a brothel. I believe that it is a testimony to my calling as a minister that when prompted to pray at the funeral, I prayed a stirring testament to my father-in-law and his memory, so much so that many of the local preachers, obviously unaware of my condition, invited me to preach at their churches. My response to these invitations was a very polite, "I would love to!" followed by an internal desire for death.

CHAPTER 14
OH SHIT, I'M FAT

Now after my father-in-law's funeral, my wife opted to stay in Kentucky for a few months. Initially following the funeral, I was full of renewed vigor and hope for the future. This state lasted approximately three days and was quickly replaced by a fear of life that surpassed even the prior funeral state. However, this time, I had two rams in the bush, food and TV. It took me a while to return to the "boob toob" as I had previously given up excessive TV watching as part of my religious experience. But isolation, dejection, and dysfunction are very persuasive in convincing a person that vice with peace is preferable to virtue with torment any day of the week. My vices of choice were food and TV. Every day, I basked in the lascivious glory of lethargy and gluttony. You name it, I tried to eat it. Every hour on the hour, I was on the coach channel surfing. I loved the channels. Each show, each movie reflected another reality into which I could escape. It was sublime.

My parents every day or so would say things like, "Son, you can't just lay around doing nothing all day!" or "Son, if you don't exercise then you will have to deal with weight gain and illness." The irony of such statements is that when I was growing up, despite the dysfunction, it was my parents' work ethic that spurred me on to achievement. I would just look at them and say, "If they can do it, then so can I." But this was different. It is like in a state of illness, their tendency toward work tormented me. I simply couldn't find the functionality to "break in." I would see everyone around me functioning, and there I was in a daze, which just made me feel more isolated. It was like I was in a cloud of confusion. I knew that I was miserable, but I didn't know any way out and I couldn't express how I felt to anyone.

In May of 2001, I miraculously got a job as an analyst. I figured that maybe working would bring about some kind of involuntary recovery. It was a desperate move, but I had to take it. I didn't want to work. I was scared. But I knew that I couldn't stay in the stupor that I was in. I started on May 15, so on around May 9 I weighed myself for the first time in over a year. The scale read 267. "267," "267," "267." It reverberated in profligate anxiety. I felt like Marlon Brando in *Apocalypse Now*. "267," "267," echoed throughout my consciousness. *Oh shit, I'm fat!* is all I could think. And this time, I didn't have any motivation to change my state. I went upstairs to my parents' bathroom, turned on the tub streams, and thought about where I had made my mistake. *Eighth grade*, I thought. *That's when it all went sour. If I could just go back to eighth grade, I could avoid everything.* But the next morning, I was not in the eighth grade. I was on my parents' bathroom floor and all I felt was horror at the notion of another day. I went downstairs, poured myself some cereal, and turned on the television.

CHAPTER 15
SCREWING THE POOCH REVISITED

The thing about shame and guilt is that they know nothing of context. I remember for a long time not being able to read the verses, "If a man does not feed his family, then he is worse than an infidel." Now, given our history, that verse in context is pretty meaningless to most black men. I mean how can one put a yoke like that about one's neck when one already has a proverbial foot? And yet and still, it carries weight. It carries a lot of weight. The fact that since the summer of 1999 I have been in and out of conditions where I have been totally unable to feed my family by myself is still a source of shuddering shame. So when I was offered a job in May of 2001, even though I knew that I was totally unequipped to perform on a job, I took it. And it was everything I expected and worse.

I mean the people were all right as people go. And the work-life balance would have been superb for a healthy person. But for an individual who could barely sit still unless immersed in television, trying to sit still and actually use my brain was incomprehensible. I remember I used to rest up all afternoon and evening in front of the TV to garner strength for the upcoming day. I would sit around and do nothing all weekend, dreading the coming Monday. And I felt absolutely no sense of accomplishment in trying to work despite my condition; rather I just felt shame and dread. I dreaded losing my job because losing my job meant that I was even more of a failure than I already thought. Losing my job meant that I was an even worse burden on and embarrassment to my father than I had already accepted. I mean, losing my job was the absolute worst-case scenario. And so God just miraculously protected me. Even though it took me forever to finish assignments, even though I could no longer pray to Her, even though I could not function, somehow, every day I was able to make it to work.

Now in my healthy days, I loved public speaking, but not so in illness. I dreaded meetings. I dreaded social interaction of any type. And yet I also dreaded sitting at my desk. Now something had to give and in January of 2002 it gave. Work had become peculiarly stressful in the fall of 2001 and for the record, stress and illness *do not mix*. And so although I had wished for death on several occasions prior, I actually became suicidal for the first time in my life. I began to devise plans by which I would drink down a glass of dishwashing detergent, but then I would have misgivings like, "But what if I just destroy my stomach and end up having to live through illness and a fucked-up stomach?" Still, I poured the detergent on three different occasions and came close to drinking it down on three different occasions.

Then God gave me Christmas break. Now although I had not signed up to take any days off, I took three days off after Christmas anyway. I just decided to sit around and read classic novels. It had taken me several months to rediscover the ability to read and comprehend and I wanted to exercise it. So I just sat around reading the *Pickwick Papers* all Christmas break. Until the night of December 28. On the night of December 28, I went running, which was a miracle in and of itself, and prayed to God while running, "God, now I have come close to committing suicide three times. If you don't move soon, it will be the end of me."

That night when I got home I watched *Pearl Harbor* on video. And as I was watching the video, it occurred to me that I was at war with something. For the first time in a long time, I became aware of the fact that I was battling something. There were sinister forces that God had called me to war against. And that revelation did something to me. For the first time in more than two years, I felt the holy spirit all over me and I prayed in the spirit for the first time in a long time that night after preaching a sermon to my wife about the dark forces that got me into illness.

From that night forward, I began to recover. I would attend deliverance sessions and prayed all the time. At work, I would write down prayers concerning the tasks that I couldn't complete and the anxiety I felt all day. And I would go into the bathroom and scream at the top of my lungs for God to deliver me. Now little did I know at the time that the entire floor of my job could hear me. But I didn't care. It didn't matter. I finally had some hope and I was not going to waste it.

It was also on the job that I rediscovered a prayer style that I had previously thought was a function of illness. I coined it "the forgiving of sins" prayer style. And the way it works is that one says over and over again, "We forgive every creation in the creation for judging, we forgive every creation in the creation for refusing to forgive…" and so on and so forth. The way the prayer style works is that whatever one's sin or dysfunction, one can partner with God and stand on the truth that through the Holy Spirit one has the apostolic ability to forgive anyone of anything and forgive oneself and others for that sin or dysfunction. Whether it be cancer or AIDS or lying or masturbation or a learning disability, one can use the prayer style in addition to more traditional deliverance techniques to deal with the problem. I used it on my father's prostate cancer and though I can draw no scientifically definite conclusions, there was a parallel between his improvement and the times that I used the style.

But anyway, long story short, it was at this job, through pride and fear of failure, that I rediscovered hope. Unfortunately it was also at this job that a few too many bathroom prayer sessions and a few too long hiatuses from work aroused suspicion and I was eventually fired. But that was no matter, for I had found hope and a renewed trust in God and that was enough.

CHAPTER 16
THE TWIN THERAPEUTIC TOWERS

While I have not yet fully recovered from illness, and so am far from an authority, I believe that medicine, while indispensable to achieve stability, is of little consequence without therapy and will. For me, my faith in God provided me with will, but therapy in the beginning was another story. In the beginning of my illness, I was simply too sick to benefit from counseling. I mean if a person cannot open up and be honest about what they are experiencing, how can counseling help them? It was not until the spring of 2002 that I was ready to undergo some therapy. And therapy is what I got!

Now a big part of my improvement has been the relaxation of my theology from a "turn or burn sensibility" to a less schizophrenic conception of an all-merciful savior. So I needed one therapist to bounce theological ideas off of and another to give me the down-and-dirty truth about myself. Both were Christians, but one was a no-nonsense conservative Christian counselor, and the other was a much more liberal Catholic. Although both got on my nerves a lot, they were invaluable to my healing.

I remember sessions with them where I would foam at the mouth and spit saliva in their trash cans. I believed and still believe that the foam was like a kind of release from dark forces and so I was superstitious about swallowing it. So week after week, I would monologue with these guys and foam, and they would listen and probe.

Thinking about these two reminds me of pastors at various churches that showed me kindness. Although I am pretty staunchly liberal in my theology and politics, it was often conservative Christian charismatics that showed me the most kindness and love in the midst of illness. Kindness from unexpected places taught me a lot about categories and labels and demonstrated that there is truly good in everyone.

CHAPTER 17
HIGH ON LIGHT

All right, I promised that I would not be political. But I said nothing about theology. Theology in a phrase is the study of God. And it is my opinion that Americans do not do enough theology. What Americans often do is "judgeology." They use God as an excuse to judge others, rather than seek God with their intellects, emotions, and spirits. But let me get off my soapbox and get to the point. Bottom line, conservative Christian doctrine is schizophrenic and dangerous medicine for the unstable mind. The notion that God is love and loving and yet will condemn a significant portion of humanity is inconsistent, period! And no amount of theological gymnastics can change that fact. For the mentally unstable, the results of truly engaging the doctrines of eternal damnation and the inerrancy and infallibility of scripture can be fatal!

Bearing all this in mind, a significant part of my recovery has been embracing the more merciful and gracious notion that when Jesus died on the cross he successfully died for all people's sins and, as a result, no further price is necessary to include obligatory confession. I believe that some folks, as a function of remedial punishment, may spend some time in hell, but that time surely won't last forever! I also believe that individuals still need to give their lives to Christ, not to avoid eternal damnation, but rather to fully know God. This theology enables one to believe the best about people and other people's religions without forsaking Christ. I do not want to sell universalism, as much as I at least want to pay it homage. It enabled me to change the nature of my thinking, such that I could in good conscience hope for the best.

Now I can't act like I have arrived because I began this book talking about how I "screwed the pooch" on my internship. But the difference between now and the beginning is that now I know that I will get better, whereas before I didn't know that. Now I know that God has power over all flesh and God will heal me, whereas before I doubted it. For my destiny is the same as the destiny of all human beings who have ever existed; my destiny is to prosper!

CHAPTER 18
UNIVERSITY MAMMON

After being forced to resign at my analyst job, I started to work in sales. I loved these jobs because through them I was able to relearn my zeal for social engagement and public speaking. These jobs also seemed to generate "foam," which is always good, so I would have a trash can right by my desk and just spit saliva into it all day. Now this period was a period of exceptional improvement.

From the time that I got "anointed" back in the winter of 2002, I put my wife through her teaching certification program, finished and published the book that I had written in college called *A Book of Rhythm*, taken care of my daughter on Saturdays while my wife was in class (seems normal, but for a person in recovery it is quite a feat!), and become one of the premier analysts in a major corporate firm. And then I went and did it, I said to myself, "I'm going back to graduate school!"

Trying to get into graduate school given my work history and the fact that I could still barely keep concentration for long periods of time was truly a devastating undertaking. In fact, it was around the time that I decided to engage in the highly stressful undertaking of trying to get into graduate school that I started having "episodes." Now episodes are truly inexplicable and unique creatures. In fact, I have not yet met anyone else, healthy or ill, that has ever experienced exactly this brand of torment. This is not surprising given the fact that each person experiences mental illness differently, and so one person's set of symptoms for the same diagnosis could greatly differ from another person's.

Episodes adhere to the following process:

Stage 1—Instability
Stage 1 of an episode involves a state of being in which one feels strangely "ungrounded" and one's stomach is in a state of mild spasm.

Stage 2—Fear
Stage 2 involves quick thoughts, apprehension, anxiety, or fear about really anything ranging from whether someone has been offended by a statement that one has just made or the paranoia that one might get fired from a job for a mistake.

Stage 3—Anxiety
Stage 3 involves a breakdown of breathing and the onset of powerful anxiety characterized by a desire to flee and much more strident stomach spasms.

Stage 4—Psychotic Symptoms
Stage 4 entails the onset of psychotic symptoms in which one feels the urge to hurt oneself or others and one often hears voices from both the inside and outside, which results in the perception that one's personality is no longer in tact, but that it is actually a hodgepodge of warring and conflicting personas.

Stage 5—Abject Depression
Stage 5 of an episode is a state in which one is completely "cloudy," unable to focus, and fervently suicidal. It is often likely for one to toggle in between stage 4 and stage 5 before the episode ends.

An episode spanning from stages 1 to 5 can last anywhere from 20 minutes to 12 hours. I remember having episodes at work, and making up excuses like "I have a stomach virus" so that I could either go home, recover, and come back or so that I could go home and stay the rest of the day. Episodes are socially and structurally debilitating because one never knows when they are going to hit. As a result, one is often afraid to travel on vacation or do other things for fear that an episode will hit. In order to cope with episodes I have often taken cold showers, bit down on a sock or rolled-up notebook, paced around hitting myself in the stomach, and rubbed my head incessantly. Sometimes prayer has worked when I was able to pray, but I have rarely been able to pray in the midst of an episode.

All right, back to graduate school. Well, from the time that I decided to go back to school, graduate school became a kind of "mammon." Mammon is any object over which one idolatrously obsesses. And I tell you, I was obsessed with graduate school. I began to forgive things like "refusing to understand" and "refusing to remember" with the forgiving of sins prayer style as a way to heal my mind so that I could focus on my school work. I enrolled in a GRE course and worked obsessively. I ended up scoring a 660 on the math, a 650 on the verbal, and a 670 on the GMAT. I took the GMAT because I was tacitly considering doing a joint program in divinity and business. When I got my scores back, I felt elation like none other. I felt like going back to all those psychiatrists who had told me that my mind would never fully recover, to kiss my black ass!

Well, long story short I not only ended up getting into both divinity and business school, but I was able to convince them to allow me to construct my own joint degree in divinity and business. Why a joint degree, you ask? Well, when you're mentally ill and a universalist in a nation like America, you need all the degrees that you can possibly get!

CHAPTER 19
PARANOIA SELF-DESTROYER

Before I enter the last, graduate school, phase of the book, I would like to circumvent chronology and explore a symptom that plagued really before my illness became full-blown: paranoia. Paranoia is worth me leaving the rhythm of this memoir. Paranoia is a worthy enemy to justify leaving the memoir tone of this brief chronicle for just one chapter and enter into the arena of deliverance ministry. Paranoia is a function of perverse perception and it affects everyone. The only difference with the mentally ill is that for us, it keeps us from "looking functional."

Much of the ills of this world have been perpetrated as a result of mass paranoia. Hitler was paranoid and he deceived an entire nation into his delusion. Europeans were paranoid when they believed that Africans were inferior because they chose to dance and embrace nature rather than create guns and weapons of mass destruction. We are paranoid when we keep thinking that our wives are against us, when in actuality, they have been praying for us with abandon.

If I relay one thing with this book, it is that the single most devastating aspect of my illness even when one considers the episodes and deep depressive and manic cycles has been paranoia. Paranoia has robbed me from appreciating relationships with good people. Paranoia has caused me to be verbally abusive to at least one of my girlfriends and my wife because I believed that they were somehow "against me."

Paranoia has caused me to ruin jobs and attack people who did not deserve the way I acted toward them. In truth, much of this paranoia has stemmed from being mistreated and misunderstood at various parts of my life and the other aspects of this paranoia stem from chemical imbalance, but nonetheless paranoia has been my greatest foe. Paranoia and its reflection, delusion, are Satan's most useful weapons as she wages war on humanity.

And so, even though this is supposed to be a simple memoir and not much else, I am going to expose you to something that I have done time and time again in my journey to get free from mental illness. Here goes:

In the name of Jesus, paranoia, you have no dominion over us.

In the name of Jesus, paranoia, we rebuke you.

Paranoia, we nail you to the four corners of the cross of Christ.

We run you through with several swords of the Word of God.

We drag you out of your high places.

We drag you out of your low places.

We light the fire of mount carmel from underneath you.

Paranioa, with each passing "trilla-second," and we are defining "trilla-second" by the time it takes the earth to spin one 18 trillionth around on its axis, you are becoming smaller and less powerful on the earth.

In the name of Jesus, in the name of Jesus, in the name of Jesus!— paranoia, come out of every creature in the creation right now.

Come out of all of us and never return to any creature ever again.

In the name of Jesus, paranoia, you are vanquished and destroyed. In the name of Jesus it is so, in the name of Jesus it is so, in the name of Jesus it is so!

And Heavenly Father, Jesus, Holy Ghost, Buddha, Muhammed, Mother Mary, Council of Elders, Vishnu, Krishna, Heavenly Mother, all good saints and angels everywhere, and all good forces in the universe, please enforce what we have spoken as so, with everything that you are, everything that you have, at all times, and in all ways. In Jesus' name we touch and agree. In Jesus' name, amen.

CHAPTER 20
HEAD-RUBBING ECCENTRICITIES

Ah, we are finally here. We are finally at that Bethesda place of stress-induced healing: graduate school. The brass ring, the final stage, the final phase is upon us, *graduate school*! Ah, the coveted graduate school through which I can put my life back together. I believe that now is a good time to confide that I pretty much keep the illness a secret from most people, especially employers. You would be surprised how different people will treat you when they find out that you are mentally ill. Instead of being justifiably angry about injustice, all of a sudden one is not taking their meds. Instead of struggling with an ailment, all of a sudden one is "just feeling sorry for oneself." As a result, I have opted for several reasons to keep the illness secret in most settings. Keeping the illness secret is also a source of profound motivation; you'd be surprised what you can achieve when you're paranoid about people finding out that you're sick.

Divinity school was no different. The way my joint program is set up, I do one year in the divinity school, one year in the business school, another year in the divinity school, and then the last year in both schools. So I started out my graduate education in divinity. This was a blessing, as divinity school folks have a tendency to be more empathic; still the bitterness of living in a nation that often ignores their sensibilities leaves many "liberal Protestants" with a bit of a hard edge. But I had no problem with homosexuals and at least bestowed tacit support to feminism, so I fit in pretty well.

But I tell you the contrast between my internal state and my external image makes the phrase cognitive dissonance seem meaningless. I mean, this was a setting where I had exams, papers, maps, and reflections due. It was surreal. I was tormented from the very beginning. One way in which I attempted to fend off episodes and stay focused in class was rubbing my head. Don't ask me why it worked, it just worked. Well, ironically, given that I was pretty outspoken in my classes, people began to associate me with this "head rubbing." I mean, individuals would say things like, "Oh, don't get Jacob started thinking about justice 'cause he'll start rubbing his head." I mean, here I was struggling to survive and simply keep my mind engaged and people were attributing it to eccentric genius. Now if that ain't God's grace, I don't know what is?!

CHAPTER 21
MY NIGGAS

"My niggas" is not some crass shout out, rather it is paying homage to the forces of the universe for the people who were instrumental in some way for my recovery. Not to suggest that said recovery is complete or final, but rather to assert that without other human beings, trained and otherwise, recovery from mental illness is highly unlikely.

My niggas are people who either intentionally or unintentionally affirmed my personhood, consequently empowering me to rediscover my identity. What does this reflect? This reflects the unmitigated power of affirmation in recovery. I mean asking God to do things through me was extremely helpful in getting me off of my parents' couch, but without somebody saying, "Hey, I love you" or "You know you're very strong for enduring this illness and not giving up." I would have been in "coach potato" heaven a long time ago.

And yet, when one suffers from illness, niggas can also be quite a temptation. Paranoia does not limit itself to those who do not care about you. Paranoia attacks concerning friend and foe alike. The slightest gesture or hint toward rejection by someone that I have made myself vulnerable to has often resulted in two or three days of imbalance. This can be humiliating for men, who are often taught that vulnerability and weakness are synonymous. And yet, I declare that the benefits of having niggas, in whom one confides the ups and downs, highs and lows far outweighs the risk of rejection that one bares.

Long story short, divinity school was like a "nigga candy store" and a brother sure got his fill. To be around individuals who were like minded or at least willing to agree to disagree about God and politics and life was affirming in a way that I cannot describe. And so I won't.

CHAPTER 22
THE CIGARETTE TEMPLE INCIDENT

As affirming as it is to say the phrase "I'm a universalist" and have no one gasp, it is also incredibly taxing to argue about things theological. As a result, I had more "episodes" during my first semester in graduate school than I had in two years prior. And that is quite a few fucking episodes, let me tell you! One thing that seemed to induce episodes was a lack of sleep and of course one of the premier scarcities of graduate school is sleep. So any given day, any day no matter what, could be a day that I had to quickly excuse myself from class, drive home, and call my wife in panic and terror. This, coupled with the fact I was extremely paranoid about missing class, made for an interesting semester to say the least.

One "episode" that must go down in history as the most hilarious in reflection yet most terrifying in real time is what I like to call the "Cigarette Temple Incident." In a prior chapter I discussed "my niggas," those individuals whom I view as invaluable to my recovery. Well, late in the first semester of my first year at the divinity school, I had the opportunity to fellowship with two such brothers the night before I was scheduled to tour a Hindu temple with my Hindu-Christian Dialogue Class. Integral to this story is the fact that touring the temple was an integral aspect of the class experience and so also integral to my grade in the class. Normally, given that I had such an important appointment the following day, I would have politely declined these brothers' invitation to go out for drinks. However, given that I had a feeling about these brothers, I figured it was worth the risk.

So the night before, I was scheduled to tour the Hindu Temple, I drank a bit too much, salivated over Salma Hayek in *After the Sunset*, and went to sleep around 3:00 a.m. The following morning at 9:00 a.m., I had that imbalanced feeling in my stomach, was hearing a couple voices, and said to myself, "Oh shit, here we go!" I woke up my wife and told her that I was having the beginnings of an episode. She said, "Can you go to the temple?" to which I responded, "It doesn't matter, I'm going anyway." I went to my medications and grabbed two extra Geodon's and two extra Lithobids, drank them down with some water, took a shower, put my clothes on, and was on my way!

As soon as I got in the car, I knew it was going to be a long trip out to the temple. I was panicky and afraid to drive out of my condominium complex. I turned on some Christmas music, hoping that the distraction would calm me. No such luck. I was hearing several different voices at this point and kept having to fight off the temptation to drive off the road. I was having major stomach spasms and it felt like two or three forces of personality were trying to assume command of my consciousness. But in my mind, I knew that I had to make it to that temple. This I knew!

Now I still smoked at this point, so I got out a cigarette and started smoking it. This accomplished nothing! But then I had a eureka! I pulled out a cigarette, ate it, and then threw up out of my window. This was exactly what the doctor ordered. This ritual provided one to two minutes of spasm reprieve and mental clarity. So for the next 50 minutes to the Hindu temple, I ate my cigarettes and threw up out of my driver-side window. When I finally made it to the temple, I had to face the unfortunate reality that I couldn't just eat cigarettes in front of my professor and fellow classmates. So I took off my shoes, paid homage to Ganesha, endured torment for 15 minutes or so, and then informed my professor that I had to go home due to a stomach virus, which is actually not a complete fabrication.

Now the story should end here, right? Wrong! When I got home, the episode went into full gear. I spent eight hours going in and out of the bathroom to take cold showers and finally sleep saved me. Around 7:00 p.m. I went to sleep, woke up at 5:00 a.m. and proceeded to write the two papers that I had due the following week. What is the moral of the cigarette temple incident? If you're going to get drunk with some niggas before an important school event and you suffer with mental illness, those mother fuckers better be cool as ice!

CHAPTER 23
LYNN—THE SAGE

I have always been an avid *Star Wars* fan from the movies of the 70s and 80s to the more modern *Episodes 1, 2*, and *3*. My first semester at graduate school, I needed some serious therapy! I mean, I needed like an intervention. What I found I am not sure could be defined as therapy, but it was an intervention. I met Lynn—the Sage. Lynn Lynnox is a woman whose daughter was schizophrenic. Lynn Lynnox was like Yoda and Shirley MacLaine wrapped up into one person. She was very strange in the sense that she had books about magic and such all over her living room bookcase. In the early sessions, I had to go slowly, as hypnosis and things like that offend the traditional Christian sensibility. But the more I went, the more able to deal with episodes I became, almost as if something was happening in my subconscious outside of my conscious will.

More specifically, Lynn simply taught me how to breathe. Now I know that breathing seems pretty straightforward but it isn't. Many times life trauma or stress actually impairs our ability to breathe and actually stifles the extent to which we consciously engage breath. Lynn, through her demeanor, hypnosis, and affirmation, awakened me to breathe. This focus on breathing enabled me to stop smoking, and eventually with the help of fasting and prayer, overcome episodes. I no longer have episodes of the extreme nature as the one described in "The Cigarette Temple Incident," at least in part to Lynn's breathe training.

In addition, Lynn taught me how to re-frame my illness in different terms. She often referred to the illness as a trial rather than as a lifelong impediment. She often referred to me more as a warrior who has to be tried and tested before entering into battle than as a helpless victim. Lynn allowed me to see that though I had grown dependent on my wife in certain ways, I never abnegated my role as leader of my family and that what I endured during illness was a testimony to my strength and future potential rather than to my incompetence or cowardice. In a phrase, Lynn Lynox as a non-baptized seeker taught me as much about the Holy Spirit and His love for me as I ever learned in church.

Chapter 24
Richard Simmons for the Obsessive Compulsive

One of the advantages to being obsessive is that if one can actually focus the mind on something positive, then obsession can lead to miraculous accomplishment in the short run. Lynn's breathing training, dropping one class spring semester, God's grace, obsessive trips to the gym, a monthly regimen of Nutrisystem, and a fast that I developed combined to result in the loss of 50 pounds in three months.

The result was variegated. Number one, I developed an unprecedented narcissism where I was in the mirror every morning obsessing on whether or not I was gaining it all back. Number two, I became very popular with the ladies, which given the fact that I am married was as much of a curse as a blessing. I mean given our culture, random females checking me out was extremely affirming, yet maintaining the discipline to stay faithful in the midst of such queries was difficult. Not to mention the shame and guilt that came from just looking at people from the opposite sex in a way that was more provocative than usual was daunting. Yet just for the record, I was faithful, diligent, and dutiful to the end. The end of course being this past summer where I gained back 30 of the 50 pounds that I lost.

CHAPTER 25
BUSINESS SCHOOL—A LESSON IN FUNCTIONAL NARCISSISM

If my Richard Simmons Obsession diet was the beginning of Narcissism, my tenure in business school reflected its climax. Business school was by far my most labor- and time-intensive endeavor since maybe the military. I mean, the whole experience was predicated on the miraculous. Miraculously losing weight gave me a superhuman sense of possibility, which is key because I needed one for business school. I mean, you name the time, I was working. Three a.m, 6:00 a.m., Sunday at 6:30 a.m.! It didn't matter! I've always wondered what empowers executives to lay off mass numbers of employees without notice or what empowers them to pollute water supplies. Well, after bBusiness school I know. Those mother fuckers are too damn busy to notice their community responsibilities. I mean, when someone is working an 80-hour work week, interspersed with two to three nights of debaucherous stress relief, well one has the recipe for complete community disconnect.

My first semester of business school, I had one thing on my mind: Jacob. And the second thing on my mind was money. So I suppose that you could describe my mind as one track during first semester: "Jacob making lots and lots of money!" I was so immersed in this achievement paradigm that I didn't even notice that God had completely delivered me from those troublesome "episodes." Of course that was by necessity, as I never could have survived business school while having to contend with those God-forsaken "episodes."

Second semester demonstrates, however, that no matter how far one thinks one is beyond the help of God's intervention, He will find a way to generate the requisite humility. Struggling to find a spring internship and having to tell three of my professors about my illness due to a three-week cycle of depression humbled a nigga right quick, fast and in a hurry. This humbling brought me back to the land of the "critically conscious" and reinforced in me a sense of a God and world larger than the vanity and ego of the "Jacobman." This was a tough transition that God wrought, but a valuable one if I was going to one day "choke, choke, choke," selflessly "choke, choke," share my testimony, "choke, choke" (all right, hold on, give me a minute. I'm overwhelmed by the beauty of this altruistic act of disclosure) with the world!

CHAPTER 26
NAMI—COMING OUT OF THE CLOSET

During my second semester at business school, an unfortunate cycle of depression forced me to reach out. I was stressed and totally dysfunctional so I contacted two advocacy groups: NAMH—The National Association of Mental Health and NAMI—The National Alliance of Mental Illness. Both organizations were extremely helpful, but for no particular reason I pursued NAMI locally. NAMI's mission of advocacy and "recovery!" were affirming to the path that I had trod, and individuals within the organization were unbelievable in their insight into illness and God's role in eradicating it.

Partnering with NAMI, however, taught me something. I think that if I had ever taken the time back in 2001, when I was diagnosed with bipolar and schizoaffective disorder, to really think about the gravity and possible permanence of my condition, I don't think I would have made it this far. But my theological training taught me that with God's help and intervention, no suffering need be eternal, and where there is a will, there is motherfucking way!

NAMI taught me that while I may not be fully recovered from illness, I had come much further than I may have assessed. NAMI affirmed me into realizing that I had managed to provide for my family, maintain employment, and get into a prestigious graduate school, all while keeping my illness a secret. Through NAMI I realized that my "testimony" was powerful and that I had a responsibility to help others in a similar state. As business school has taught me to always look for the "win-win," the obvious hope is that I will recover more fully as I share what I know and have done with others.

CHAPTER 27
ALL THINGS BABY

All right, my curious companion, we are now full circle. It is now the summer of 2006. I screwed the pooch on my spring internship and am currently working as a package handler to pay the bills and stay in some modicum of physical condition. So after reading my story, do you think I'm lazy, incompetent, or simply misunderstood? Or do you find yourself questioning such categories? After reading my story, do you find yourself questioning the labels that we put on one another? I tell you after writing this memoir, I find myself questioning anything and everything that says that we can't make it. Like the big Barak says, "Yes we can!" I tell you, after writing my story, I find myself questioning everything and anything that contends that there is any good thing under God that is not possible through God.

I mean, bottom line, I still get paranoid. I still feel paralyzed sometimes. I still get depressed. But there is a difference between now and 2001. Now I know that those bouts won't remain. Now I know that God loves me enough to heal me. It's important that you pay attention to this last chapter 'cause, yo, you could lose the whole vision if you're not careful.

In the summer of 2001, I couldn't run a mile. Now I run four miles three times a week. In the summer of 2001, I couldn't read or focus. Now I am in an elite graduate school doing a joint program that I created. In the summer of 2001, I weighed 280 pounds and couldn't stand the sight of myself. Now I weigh 250 and though I have a potbelly, I still look at my muscles in the mirror ad nausem. In the summer of 2001, I wished that my wife and daughter would die. Now I pray fervently each day for their safety. In the summer of 2001, I saw no hope to do ministry ever again. Now I am doing a ministry internship en route to ordination. See, my brother and sister, this shit is possible.

The biggest deception that the "enemy" ever perpetrated against humanity isn't that he doesn't exist; it's that he's powerful enough to stifle the miraculous and life-giving grace of God. Yo, with God, there is nothing that we can't do. All things, baby! Say it with me. "All things are possible with God!" Say it again, "All things are possible with God!" Yeah, I may still have problems focusing sometimes. And yeah, paranoia still afflicts a brother. But yo, bottom line, I will get this degree! I will graduate in May and go on to lead a highly functional life! Because God is with me, and that's enough!

CHAPTER 28
THE PhD PROLOGUE

It is now the summer of 2007. I managed to graduate from both my business school and divinity school programs in May of 2007 and won an award to boot! I also managed to get into a PhD program studying social entrepreneurship. It turns out that those business school guys weren't so narcissistic after all, and that quite a few of them really want to help people. Why more school? Well, I figured that if school had brought me this far, then school still had some blessings of recovery yet. I also started a chapter of NAMI on my campus, a feat for which I am exceptionally proud, given that it was kind of a pain in the ass. I am starting to tell my story and am inspiring some folks as I do it. I am anxious about starting the PhD program, but I figure that God has brought me this far, and he'll keep on keepin' on. I have also affiliated with a church home with a pastor who is, in a phrase, "the coolest motherfucker in ministry!"

CONCLUSION

The boy finished reading the notebook teary eyed. He said, "Wow, Granddaddy, I never knew how hard it was for you. All those books you've written, all those companies you helped start, all those students you've taught. I never would have thought that you had to overcome so much."

Grandaddy Jacob responded, "Joseph, I'm sorry that I waited so long to tell you my story. 'Cause it doesn't belong to just me. All of us, Joseph, all of us must overcome something in this life. And now I hope you understand why you can't ever give up, beloved. You can't ever give up 'cause when you hold on till the end, God will come up with something. I know it feels like in these dark times that God doesn't care anymore. Remember, Joseph, the belief of one person, just one person, can change a generation."

"Wow, Grandaddy, do you think I can really make things better?" Joseph said.

"I know it. I know that you and those like you will. And that's the end. The end is the beginning 'cause all this suffering is just a dream of insanity, a dream waiting for us to wake up, to new beginnings of joy," Grandaddy Jacob responded.

And with that, Joseph grabbed Jacob's hand and they began to pray. And they kept praying, joining their voices with the voices of the suffering, the bereft, the noble, and lowly too. And they prayed until all things were renewed and the world knew redemption.

Amen.

Printed in the United States
112036LV00004B/34/P